Mickey Mouse
and the Bicycle Race

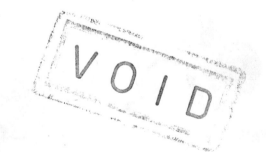

Walt Disney's
Mickey Mouse
and the Bicycle Race

Written by Cindy West
Illustrated by Sharon Ross

A Golden Book • New York
Western Publishing Company, Inc., Racine, Wisconsin 53404

"A race!" said Mickey Mouse.
"We should have
a bike race."

Mickey and Goofy
got on a bike.
Donald and Daisy
got on another bike.

"One, two, three…
GO!"
said Minnie.
They were off!
Two bikes raced fast
down the hill.

"Stop! Stop!" said Goofy.
"Where is my
lucky penny?"
One bike stopped.

"Here it is!"
said Goofy.
"Now we can go."
They were off!
Two bikes raced fast.

"Stop! Stop!"
said Goofy.
"I have to eat.
I have to be strong
for the race."
One bike stopped.

"Now we can go,"
said Goofy.
They were off!
Two bikes raced fast.

"Stop! Stop!"
said Goofy.
"I must read my book.
I must read
about racing."
One bike stopped.

"Now we can go,"
said Goofy.
They were off!

"Faster!" said Mickey.
"We must catch up."
"I am going as fast
as I can," said Goofy.

Donald and Daisy
were still ahead.
"Do not give up,"
said Mickey.
"Never," said Goofy.

"We are next to them,"
said Mickey.
"We can win.
We can win the race!"

"Stop! Stop!"
said Goofy.
"No! No!"
said Mickey.
"Not now."

"Yes! Yes!"
said Goofy.
"Now.
Look at Ferdie.
He looks so sad."
One bike stopped.

"I lost my new kite,"
said Ferdie.
"I lost it
in that tree."

"We will get your kite,"
said Mickey.
Mickey and Goofy
got the kite.

Mickey and Goofy
got back on
the bike.

"I hope you win
the race," said Ferdie.

Mickey and Goofy
rode very fast.
But they could not
catch Daisy and Donald.

"We won!" said Donald.
"We won!" said Daisy.
Minnie gave them
each a prize.

Mickey and Goofy
smiled at Donald
and Daisy.
They began
to go.

"Stop! Stop!"
said Minnie.
"I have prizes
for you two.

"It is a prize
for being good friends
to Ferdie."
"We are winners, too!"
said Goofy.
"Yes, you are,"
said Minnie.

Then they all
took a ride
together.